An Ode to The Mac

I feel ya 100% Mac
How an Instagram Pic
make you get a 6pack
Or how mention of a name
Gotcha taking Shots to the brain .
And it really really hurts .
While they standing there with a smirk .
And some reason you keep itching
Cuz you on 2 and a half percs .
And they don't understand
just expect you to move on.
And they next chapter starting
But you still holding on.
I feel you my nigga
The thought of a new nigga .
Kicking incredibly dope shit
And she won't chose you nigga .
And already got another
that shit kinda foul.
A whole fifth of henny and about 90 Miles
Prally make it feel a whole lotta better .
Heartbreaks will kill ya if you let her.
Don't listen to the sympathetics
"You will find better"
"You gone get something new"
Because I'm tryna spend my days with you
But hey we guys we supposed to take it on the chin .
But it ain't no sympathy for a heart broken man.

Happy Thanksgiving

Can ya tell me that you love me girl ?
Even though I lie I still adore you girl.
Cuz yeah a nigga lie but my intentions be good.
Ion need ya worrying more than ya should .
Can ya tell me that you love me?
Cuz I can't tell .
The thought you without me is like Keenan no Kell.
SpongeBob with no snail.
I remember that episode and SpongeBob was sick as hell
Cuz he felt like that he really took somebody's love for granted .
And when it's was gone he couldn't stand it .
Even though we both know we were dead wrong.
We still just want ya to come back home.
Cuz not hearing ya voice make the days draw long .
Compiled with the other bullshit going on.
Just hear me out baby I know I fucked up.
But it was times ya hurt me too but I had to suck that shit up . But space what ya need and space Whatchu get. Hmu girl happy thanksgiving

Mr. Slick

Mr. slick Mr. Slick
how could you be so smooth?
How you can say one thing
But never front your move?
How once before you
were a regular dude
And now you're known as.
Mr. Knockin them Boots?
Mr. Slick Mr. Slick .
They will never know .
Of the love that you were
to trying to dish out before .
But they were sleep
Now you're meat to meat
And before you're asleep
The memories will delete .
Mr. Slick Mr. Slick or
Mr. lead them on .
It's a shame they'll never know
of a love so strong .
All because you were loved
so so wronged
And you were the great guy
those other chicks gave up on.

A Crush

Oh woman oh woman .
I love how you keep it G.
So cool and kind
And as fine as can be.
Green eyes
Skin so divine.
In love with the thought
Of you staying on my mind.
Don't you ever get turned off
By the things you hear .
Cuz I was living my life
Before I drifted here .
And I notice how you drifted here too.
I guess Mr whathisname
Ain't know what to do.
And I know you know about me being a Que.
And all the mannish things you heard we do
And I had practice just for pleasing you
With hopes of permanently appeasing you

Courting

This is new to me so
don't think it's the usual.
I can help get ya hair done
Or help fix ya cuticles.
Pay for the whole check
Eat it up without reciprocals
And won't sweat a thang
Cuz we having plenty more.
So don't trip when
I'm inclined to take a trip
Or make reservations
For a paint and sip .
Or buy ya nice things
That cost a grip.
Or even the small things
Like extra Pibb .
Cuz it's all just a token
For being the coldest.
A token to all those
Flings that left ya broken.
A token to damn girl yo body smokin
A token to you having me
write this late night with no stroking
mhmhm yo fine ass girl
Well back to the poem I had a lil moment .
I'll buy ya the world if it was a price on it .
And if I was broke I'll try to steal it for ya baby .
I couldn't stop loving you if they paid me
So don't you hurt me like the rest of them do.
Even though I'll never compare them to you
I just want you to know what I've been through
And all the Loses that brought me to you

Sex on The First Date

You can have options
But only one right .
It could take 90 days
Or it could take one night

And that ain't gon change
The time that get spent .
Cuz sex is good
But I really love ya scent .

I really love ya smile girl
How it compliment ya face .
And I love ya lips
And how ya other lips taste .

So sex is cool
But we can take our time
Cuz nothing substitutes
Digging into ya mind

And I know I know
how this thang go .
"You too good to be true"
"You're leaving fasho"

Let's not forget the
"Oh I heard all that before"
Well before me, it was
squares at ya door

And you need to recognize
when the win at ya hand
Cuz I can be myself
And still get into ya pants .

8 Letters 3 Syllabus

I Love you
About 8 letters
Used the right way
can make her wetter
Used too early
Could make her fear
The real reasons that brought you here
And the feelings that got her here
And the guys who said it in previous years.
And that right there may shake her up
Cuz the same words used before brought her bad luck
With other guys
telling lies
And reeling her back With love in disguise.
Used too late
Well you can't escape
The guilt and hindsight that you may face
Of another guy
In yo panty pie
And teaching their kids how to multiply
When you were that guy
That she was planning with all this time
But you were too cool just to let those 8 letters fly.
Used right on time
Shid what's right on time ?
When you married in a suit
Throwing Rice like Dilfer dimes?
When You fuck the first night feeling butterflies?
When you broke and she offers you five guys ?
When dilated and contractions happening untimed?
Well your guess is as good as mine.
I feel like I done been in love several times.
And every time was something different
Only thing that was the same
Was my internal feelings.
And I can just say tell them regardless of that .
Cuz I love Yous are something that you can't take back.

FriENDS

Friends are here for experiences.
Nothing more nothing less
You have them forever
Or have them for less
But the experiences you have
Hold them near and dear
So when friends part the earth
You can have great tears
And none of regret
Cuz who want that
When you remembering friends
That you can never get back.
So be a friend
Make them grin
Cause sooner or later
All great things come to an end.
A Friend.

Hooked on Phonics

If you hurt me, I'd prally run back to you.
Run faster than a sprinter.
Run faster than a than the camera man from cheaters.
Run faster than ya stomach the morning after cheap liquor.
Run faster than a heartbeat at 6flags.
Run faster than rapper through 10 freaky thots pants.
Excuse my language babygirl that was kinda vulgar.
You da only head I want laying on my shoulders
Netflix and chill rock harder than a boulder.
Bend ya all up like a folder.
But now you occupied with ya new fling and won't come over.
Shid I hope ya new nigga treat ya right.
You got my number if he don't ever beat it right?
You gon call me just to come eat it right?
Cuz I would and Yeen gotta take no wood.
I'm here cuz I wanna make ya feel good.
Even if it's only for a moment
And even if this love ain't the strongest.
Shid even if this ain't even love .
I still cherish every kiss, dap, and hug.
You can still call when ya kids need help with algebra.
Them the pros and cons of ya Fallin for a dub.

Spark

How do you get back to feeling these women?

After all of the times you were defeated and finished?

After you gave your all, and answered every call?

How do you keep it playa and still try to be involved with attempting
to court and get to know these souls who have no intention of
attempting to grow old?

Even when you try and be the good guy?

But everytime you let your feelings fly

they get disregarded and you don't know the reasons why.

And now it's to the point where you can't even feel

and you just trying to will yourself into something that's real .

And will it ever happen? I'm not so sure but

we all hope for feelings of smiling ear to ear and

trusting someone's daughter with no fear of looking like a clown out
here .

If you have the answers, please me know

because we all lookin for someone to nurture and grow

with together but women feelings change just like the weather

and you can only be respected if you havin some cheddar.

But please help me get back to liking and hoping things go right

because I mean who's trying to be single for the rest of their life.

Pandora

What that box feel like?
I would love to know.
Do I drive fast or should I drive slow?
Rush to start? Or go head to toe?
Go for hours ? Or smash and dash?
How many other gents done hit that ass?
How many dudes yo age done been your dad?
How many broken hearts lie in your past?
Girl you selling dreams . Or you say Whatchu mean ?
Do you only want the head? Or can I touch ya spleen ?
Shid this just a conversation.
An interview before I start penetration.
Asthmatic so excuse the ventilating
But damn how many Been here before me?
Did they pay with they time or did they have a fee?
Did they take you on dates or did they hit it for free?
Would you bless them rooks if ya ran into me?
Because me the best Fuck the rest.
Did Cupid hit your heart or did ya wear ya vest ?
Who was ya best? and who was the flex?
Don't worry after this you giving that neck.
No neck? Well no sex? All them answers baby I ain't even pressed .
I wouldn't touch with a rake .
For pete's sake!
All them looks and they all for free ?
All them looks can't be for me

Passionate People

Passionate people tend to come in first
Striving and doing work
While others hurt
And hard work tend to expose perps
People who tend to go hard in spurts .
But you gotta have patience
And also be kind
And be a sovereign learner
And make use of your time
And most of all stay true to you
So you know what type of things you will not do.
Cuz people tend to get worked up and caught up in the dollar
And end up being doctors working in a parlor.
And who wanna be somebody educated and misplaced.
And all this things tend to lead to success .
So wake up in the morning and do your best .
And what's not for you leave for the rest .
Find your way and tackle every test
Cuz one day somebody else will be next
And you will be in a position to help their stress
Jah Bless

Dream Sold and Deferred

Forreal forreal
Tell me how you'd feel
If I kissed, you
And told you I'm not your Nigga forreal.
That I've been here for over year
Just to court ya and fuck ya
and leave ya right there?
Prally be mad prally
be sad prally stab me up
But I'd live cuz I'm full of good luck.
But hey how could you place blame
when ya feelings changed
I stopped juugin and stopped having change
And you went ghost and your lip poked
In your friends' group messages
you was telling good jokes.
All in hopes for us to elope.
But not so fast
you don't get a pass
Same girls sharing a laugh
With me in a bath.
Eating shrimp steaks and crabs
And that get back real believe it or not
Have ya eyes swollen and noses pouring with snot.
Chasing another guy that you think is sweet and loving.
Not knowing he having alternative plots.
In pursuit of the same things, that I was honest about
Now, you hurt heartbroken lip poking out
On Instagram tryna dish and air him out.
Cuz you damaged and tryna gain some clout
Man please.
You can't be mad, that's the fee
For disrespecting the King that was keeping it G.
Buying Shopping sprees and telling you
"Baby you not the one for me"
And All that hate you projected on AP?
And now you sick, hurt, fucked on,
and looking like a goofy

1>60

You fuckin 50 niggas tryna figure out why my shit so bomb
50 niggas touched it and ain't make you cum and you sitting
around banking on number 51
And now you sick he ain't get the Job done .
That thought of it prally eating you up .
Getting drunk at the bar now they beating you up.
Leaving you stuck
Like "WHAT DA FUCK"
"WHY AP THE BADDEST MAN TO DIG IN THESE GUTS ? "
51 52 53 54 55
How many more niggas getting in between ya thighs?
Telling you lies saying "I'm that guy"
And you let them slide and they buss in 5
Mins or less and now you stressed cuz you let another nigga popped
and you ain't cum yet?
56 57 58 59?
Now you think you can change yo mind?
About all them times you could've been mine but you declined for a
couple neverminds?
Like I'm inclined to lose like that
And cuff up 1000 other niggas go to smack?
When you figured out they the ones who lack
The essentials during sex cuz my shit like crack. And

 I broke the world record for broken backs.

Creating the cheat code for making Coochie's sound like Mac.

And having women run back to back

After 6 years with some other weak fella

she chose for the prematurely artificial betters.

He can have more cheddar,

BUT HE CAN'T GET YOU WETTER.

Backdoor Bandit

Oh man Oh man
There's a bad man there .
Chocolate Skin
Jet black curly hair .
Have no fear .
As we shed a tear .
For all the relationships
You fixed this year .
When she ain't want it to end
But just needed break cuz
Her man don't know
how to make her shake
Now she a midnight steak
And I Must say
I don't see how sex and love equates
Backdoor Bandit
Boyfriend #2
How many other guys chicks
Have you slid into?
"But imma good guy
I always give her back!"
"When he in town
I don't even text her back!"
That's a fact
But look at it like this
How would you feel
if they backdoored ya chick?
You might be sick
Might Not give a shit
But a lotta trust issues
Comes with It .
Now you won't even cuff a chick
Or even give one the benefit of the doubt
All because you in and owt
Another man's spouse.

21 Questions Gone Left

If I were your heart baby would let me beat?
If I came home famish, would you let me eat?
Do you get one ring or did you 3peat?
3 peat? So, I guess you got it made.
Booty call hours and I guess you getting laid.
Only difference is that you laying with some lames.
I'll never give a freak a diamond ring.
But freak is definitely subjective.
Cuz we all would be hoes if a broken heart judged us.
But we gotta choice in this world to pursue happiness.
Even if happiness lies in just me clapping it.
And whatever we gotta do
From spending time and consensual sexual conquest schemes
Ain't nothing wrong if my happiness lies inside them jeans.
Same way your happiness lies in diamond rings.
You could definitely hold out and not let me make ya cling.
Cuz this right here some bomb jimmy dean.
The type of loving that'll make you mean.
And slander my name if we ain't want the same things.

Down Below

When ya down look around
And tell me Whatchu see?
A whole space around me.
Ain't no hoes
Ain't no Bros
All yeses
No No's
Just a lotta leprechaun's tryna steal a nigga gold.
But don't get discouraged let it keep you from ya goals.
You big man on campus if they looking at ya soul.
But they don't see that
Or maybe they just over look it.
Or maybe they see it and get shooken.
Shaken shooken this ain't English class.
Why does the good get treated so bad?
And I mean the real good not the ones out here faking.
It's all about status that gets the penetrating.
And ya niggas here only for reasons.
To stay hipped to da nigga that's gon be the reason
Or to drop salt on ya like seasons
But shit get cool when you up
Just gotta remember they don't give a fuck.
Or you might fall back for they tricks
Just a lotta nobodies tryna ride ya dick.

GOOD GUY PLIGHT

I'm in a world where ya got it or ya don't.
I'm in a world where every need is a want.
I'm in a world where they do but they don't
I'm in a world where they trying to make you believe it's cool
 to do everything that YOU please to do.
Well let me say something about that though.
Fucking 15 men may not make you a hoe.
And I understand these our selfish years I know.
But what about the dude that liked you for you though?
Shid he waited after dinner for the cookies.
He wanted some of soul before he delivered dicking.
He became a little exposed.
Told you about his goals.
Even Bought lies that you sold.
Even pictured both parties in love and old.
So, what is it really?
because y'all don't understand
The plight of the good man.
When you "Just too good to be true"
When it's easy for people just to quit on you.
And move on fast when you're still connected by a latch.
Cuz right now you're too broke to even cover the tax.
Because your skin ain't filled with tats.
And because dropping bars on wax?
So whatchu gon say when he makes it?
Then you gon rush to get naked?
But instead treat you like the last piece of bacon.
Leave you on da stove Just to letchu get cold.
The same way you did when we was 20 Years old.

Stack Yo Paper

I tried to tell you about how it goes .
You ain't listen and now yo heart broke
About how you was seen as a dollar sign
But now you broke and now you're never mind
And you sick don't know how it happened
You fell victim to all of the cappin.
Making it and splurging
And not putting it up
Strip club visits and you was fuckin it up
That time you said "Fuck Jack Daniels
Bring the patron"
All them hoes in the section won't answer the phone
They all gone and you by yo self
You ain't ate in 3 days and can't get any help
All the free game and sauce that helped niggas eat .
And you thought them niggas would put you back on ya feet?
I'm hope you learn and do better next time around
So you ain't moping around with this unbearable frown.
Tricking off on these hoes at every single lounge
And you done went broke and feel like a clown .
And you not the first and you not the last
Spending it all just to get some ass?
But you was just tryna get the heart
And made it worth they time
But you crashed and burned and then fell on yo face .
But it's cool cuz you'll be back
Can't buy these hoes shit not even a snack and that's real.

Legacies

100 years from now what's gonna be your story?

We're you the cluchest guy ever like Robert Horry?

Or did you save your peers and put them on to new things?

Managing their finances and investing

And saving and not gambling on dice games and

put a price for your face to be in places with people that's paying

And be able to touch a world of people

and understand that pain heals when it feels

that you are not equal to people who are ahead

while you're hanging on a ledge cuz tomorrow

has a different story ahead about you treading ahead?

and accumulating this bread and making it spread

for harder days instead of making it rain and

popping bottles unless it's a celebration

And I mean a real celebration for days you was broke

and other gentleman were hating

And. Now roles reversed cuz you was keeping it playa

 and now everyday there after you remembered forever.

Preach.

The CurveBall

Being complacent instead of elevating levels.

Being in da basement instead of on pedestals.

Tied down with Baggage with ya whole life ahead of you.

It's like you got da answers to da final which coulda gave you the A

But you'd rather cram and fail it on the next day.

It's like you gotta million-dollar ticket!

But rather clock into Waffle House to make hash browns on a skillet.

Stiff on a thinking man for da man that's dealing.

Rather buy into sold dreams instead of genuine feelings.

Don't save her for me cuz I ain't willing to get some leftovers when you

coulda been winning.

When ya was just as great then as you are now.

Regardless of the titles and the money piles.

You neglected my needs when I couldn't smile.

You kicked me when I was down and sleeping on a couch.

So, don't try to come around now cuz I'm having clout.

Look at the bright side. Now you all in movies now.

All these ain't shit lady's role shows whatchu about.

Blockbusters and I bet ya looking stupid now.

And I ain't spiteful in the least bit I promise.

The Thought of Us now would prally make me vomit.

Cuz what I look giving jewels to fool?

When ya had the choice to win and ya chose to lose?

When ya was jam packed for me but flexible for dude?

Yea thought so Girl you got me Bent.

Walking round here acting like ya heaven sent.

Now ya looking for some help just to pay da rent Ha.

This is a blank page dedicated to the great people that made this amazing. My momma, my father, my daughter Ava, Dr. Bass who pushed my transparency and confidence to produce this content, and to my LBs, Young Ralf who at Duke Med School right now, and Trent my Quarterback, who dream is to be a firefighter. Yall make me amazing, and I love yall. For sure. Also to the Que Psi Phi Fraternity. Yall saved my life and taught me discretion so Roo to the Great bruhz.

20/20 Hindsight Vision

Now back then we discussed been slept on .

Being your whole world and getting crept on .

Wasting ya energy like a light left on

Cuz you trying to be a shoulder to get wept on.

Like you had a chance to win the game

now you getting swept home

you chose to go to overtime

instead of take the kick

All Because you saw Nick

lose on the Kick 6

Got beat deep when you sent the blitz

Threw it on the one and threw a pick ?

But what about all them times having guts payed off

Wanting to quit follow dreams

But instead you stayed then got layed off .

And having hindsight never ever pays off.

So take a chance on the things in life that can't be bought.

B.D.E

A moment of silence for all the girls that think they was working
they moves.
When they ran into a gentleman dude.
Who was extra cool, played by the rules, put ya on game and helped
with your school.
Not because he had it because we always have it .
And to do it for every girl is just madness .
But the ones we fold for, are chasing rappers on tour.
Tickets on the floor hoping that they score.
But my heart just pours and spews out love .
Paying for all ya friends access in the club .
Just to get dubbed and shown no love
and just to see you done fell for a scrub.
Sheesh the world we live in oh so cruel .
When you infatuated and you gotta play the fool .
To know you getting milked
and still let it happen just because
you wishing that something else happens.
And it ain't no pressure you just kind of feel lesser.
Cuz you was only tryna elevate levels
And it's cool cuz this the 4th time this year .
You was chasing love and you let it interfere
with the dreams and goals, you had prior to here.
And you flyer than him with way more charm

but you only good for Watchu putting on her arm.
It's cool my nigga cuz Watchu look like clutching ?
Then all the money shit popping you just look like you bluffing but
it's nothing .
100 for nails 300$ just to eat some snails
passing out weed and you ain't use no scales
But at night you letting off wails
cuz you hurting nobody wanna get to know that person.
That's hurting and really in need of nurturing .
But you a baller nigga so you keep on purchasing
anything you need every time I feed
you then I could never leave you if I needed to because I'm hooked.

The Rebound

You ain't thinking about me?

Well vice versa I guess it's mutual

I got rid of you and bounce back with 2 of em.

One Finna be a doctor. The other engineer .

And they both let me get the throat

Like I cut em ear to ear.

So I have no fear about being forgotten.

When in reality I'm the ONLY reason you poppin.

Team Jordan to Raf?

Who taught you that?

If I could refund free game I'd take it all back.

Destiny's child and baby you Michelle .

I was jammed up and you ain't even post my bail?

Needed help on a project and ya ass let me fail?

And ya box dryer than a 1700s well.

Speaking of Wales I gotta trip there and I know you sick.

The only trips ya take is to take some dick.

I cooked I cleaned and massaged ya feet.

It's honor when ya say yeen thinking about me.

Rather it be Frank Ocean than ya sorry ass.

Druggie ass pop more bars than Alcatraz

And the sad thing is you gotta piece of me .

Should've turned plan A into Plan C

Pulled out in ya weave so we don't need plan B.

Shid speaking of plan B? How many ya skipped 3???

How many daddies they got? Between 13?

Girl you sorry better call Maury.

Got the nerve to be saying yeen thinking about me.

All Strings Attached

If I miss ya baby girl can I call you?

If the cup runeth over can I stalk you?

If I were hurting baby would ease my pain?

If I I'm fiending for it would you tease me babe?

Would you change for some fame?

Comb my beard rub my back just to keep me sane.

Let me see your pain?

Let me kiss ya forehead while we watch the game?

Kiss my T-shirts just to leave em with stains?

If you gained weight, baby can I love you in Lane's?

Take me outta my lane?

Fuck with another lame cuz he having sum change?

Would you let me touch ya body if you ain't in the mood?

Can we record it? And upload it to HQTube?

If it ain't what I thought I wanted; would you allow me to move?

And not be subjected to slander for being an honest dude?

If I had some insecurities can I trust you to remember?

Cuz I been hurt I don't want to compare you to any of them.

If I couldn't buy you meal and was forced to steal would you keep it real, and

weather the storm so the two of us can build?

I wanna know baby cuz I can't really tell

Cuz when times get a lil rough you tend to bail.

And I don't know how to not want you woman.

So, if ya could just ya know let the kid know.

So, I can get back to loving ya from head to toe.

Ceiling to floor

A blunt and a 4

And let our souls dance with one another Til their legs get sore.

The BluePrint

Do I gotta drop salt?
Or do I gotta sell dreams?
Should I try to get to know you?
Or try you like the squeeze?
Are you Gladys Knights?
Or are you Mickey D's.
Do you want me for my time?
Or do I just satisfy ya needs?
because It seems to me that you ain't tryna stay down.
When I get up. I bank that you might be around.
But if not, that'll be even better.
because I'll buy new memories to try and forget her.
And I ain't spiteful.
Even though you had me gone.
Thoughts of "when you not with me are you really alone? "
Is this mine or ya friend's cologne?
Or does this belong to somebody who was laying the bone?
Well shid I can't trip ya actions explain a lot.
I think it's me just caught up in this crazy plot;
Of you being mine and the vice versa,
You want me to never ever ever hurt ya.
And all my insecurities that I might've been blessed with.
But when I told you, they started feeling like a weapon.
Just a way for you to get cake and eat it too.
But ain't no telling how many soul ties came with you.
Well shit let me know cuz I already got an idea.
If you fuck with me, why can't I ever see ya?
Why can I only come thru When I'm having sativa?
Why your phone on mute when it's on the speaker?
Why it's a "maybe" or "we'll see" when I wanna treat ya?
Well shid you say "it's nothing" then it's cool.
Sorry about being such a fool.
But that's kind of foul watchu put me through.
Get me out my comfort zone and I really start to fuck with you.

Expose you to stuff I don't normally do.
Just to do the same thing the others do.
That's crazy.
Say you selfish
And say you ain't ready.
Like I'm supposed to make it and forget you left me.
Like I'm supposed to forget that you flexed me.
When you blessed the other guys, but you ain't bless me.
Shid but guess what it ain't no pressure though.
If I wanna rekindle flames baby, I'll letchu know.
When I wanna dab in the cookie jar.
Imma text you though.
Best believe if you become mine, imma feel sketchy though.
If not; best believe imma miss you though